W9-AHJ-676

SWEET DREAMS, CLOWN-AROUNDS!
To librarians, parents, and teachers:

Sweet Dreams, Clown-Arounds! is a Parents Magazine READ ALOUD Original — one title in a series of colorfully illustrated and fun-to-read stories that young readers will be sure to come back to time and time again.

Now, in this special school and library edition of *Sweet Dreams, Clown-Arounds!,* adults have an even greater opportunity to increase children's responsiveness to reading and learning — and to have fun every step of the way.

When you finish this story, check the special section at the back of the book. There you will find games, projects, things to talk about, and other educational activities designed to make reading enjoyable by giving children and adults a chance to play together, work together, and talk over the story they have just read.

For a free color catalog describing Gareth Stevens' list of high-quality books, call 1-800-341-3569 (USA) or 1-800-461-9120 (Canada).

Parents Magazine READ ALOUD Originals:

Golly Gump Swallowed a Fly
The Housekeeper's Dog
Who Put the Pepper in the Pot?
Those Terrible Toy-Breakers
The Ghost in Dobbs Diner
The Biggest Shadow in the Zoo
The Old Man and the Afternoon Cat
Septimus Bean and His Amazing Machine
Sherlock Chick's First Case
A Garden for Miss Mouse
Witches Four
Bread and Honey
Pigs in the House
Milk and Cookies
But No Elephants
No Carrots for Harry!
Snow Lion
Henry's Awful Mistake
The Fox with Cold Feet
Get Well, Clown-Arounds!
Pets I Wouldn't Pick
Sherlock Chick and the Giant
 Egg Mystery
Cats! Cats! Cats!

Henry's Important Date
Elephant Goes to School
Rabbit's New Rug
Sand Cake
Socks for Supper
The Clown-Arounds Go on Vacation
The Little Witch Sisters
The Very Bumpy Bus Ride
Henry Babysits
There's No Place Like Home
Up Goes Mr. Downs
Bicycle Bear
Sweet Dreams, Clown-Arounds!
The Man Who Cooked for Himself
Where's Rufus?
The Giggle Book
Pickle Things
Oh, So Silly!
The Peace-and-Quiet Diner
Ten Furry Monsters
One Little Monkey
The Silly Tail Book
Aren't You Forgetting Something, Fiona?

Library of Congress Cataloging-in-Publication Data

Cole, Joanna.
    Sweet dreams, Clown-Arounds! / by Joanna Cole ; pictures by Jerry Smath. -- North American library ed.
        p. cm. -- (Parents magazine read aloud original)
    Summary: After an exciting and busy day, the Clown-Around family has trouble getting Baby to go to bed.
    ISBN 0-8368-0976-9
    [1. Clowns--Fiction. 2. Bedtime--Fiction.] I. Smath, Jerry, ill. II. Title. III. Series.
[PZ7.C67346Sw 1993]
[E]--dc20
                                                                                        93-13038

This North American library edition published in 1994 by Gareth Stevens Publishing, 1555 North RiverCenter Drive, Suite 201, Milwaukee, Wisconsin 53212, USA, under an arrangement with Parents Magazine Press, New York.

Text © 1985 by Joanna Cole. Illustrations © 1985 by Jerry Smath. Portions of end matter adapted from material first published in the newsletter *From Parents to Parents* by the Parents Magazine Read Aloud Book Club, © 1989 by Gruner + Jahr, USA, Publishing; other portions © 1994 by Gareth Stevens, Inc.

Printed in the United States of America

1 2 3 4 5 6 7 8 9 99 98 97 96 95 94

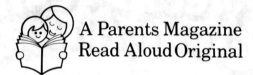

A Parents Magazine
Read Aloud Original

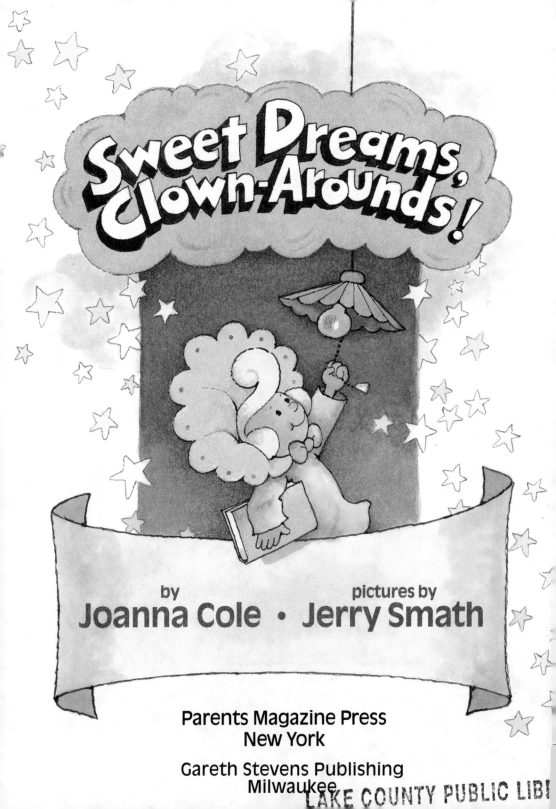

Sweet Dreams, Clown-Arounds!

by
Joanna Cole · **Jerry Smath**

pictures by

Parents Magazine Press
New York

Gareth Stevens Publishing
Milwaukee

To Imogen—J.C.

To Kyle and Kendall Stratton—J.S.

It was a happy day
for Baby Clown-Around.

She went to the supermarket
with Mr. Clown-Around.

11

She went to the shoe store
with Mrs. Clown-Around.

She played with her
big sister, Bubbles,

and with Wag-Around, the dog.

Now it was Baby's bedtime.
Mr. Clown-Around fed her supper.

Mrs. Clown-Around helped her
brush her teeth.

And Bubbles and Wag-Around
kissed her good night.

But Baby had had such
a happy day that she
did not want to go to sleep.

So she played a trick
on the Clown-Arounds.

"Where is Baby?"
Mrs. Clown-Around
asked.

Mrs. Clown-Around looked
in her teacup.
Baby was not there.

Mr. Clown-Around looked
in his shoe.

And Bubbles looked in the fishbowl.
But they could not find Baby.

Then Wag-Around followed his nose.
There was Baby!

"Now it is really bedtime,"
said Mrs. Clown-Around.

She tucked Baby in.

But Baby did not go to sleep.
"Wah, wah!" she cried.

Mr. Clown-Around rocked
the cradle,
but it didn't help.

Wag-Around sang a lullaby,
but that woke Baby up
even more.

Mrs. Clown-Around looked for
an extra blanket in the closet,
but that made things worse than ever.

Even Bubbles couldn't
put Baby to sleep.

27

All at once,
Baby reached out her hands
and said, "Bear!"

"No wonder she can't sleep!"
said Mr. Clown-Around.

He rushed out...

and brought back
a big bear.

But Baby didn't want it anymore.
"Monkey!" she said.

"She needs a monkey too!"
said Mrs. Clown-Around.
Mrs. Clown-Around rushed out...

and came back with a monkey.

But Baby didn't want it.
"Horse!" she said.

"I know where to get one,"
said Bubbles.

By the time Bubbles
came back with the horse,
Baby had stopped crying.

She was reading
a good-night book to herself.

36

Mr. Clown-Around
listened to the story,
and his eyes began to close.

Baby turned out the bright light.
It was so restful in the dark,
that Mrs. Clown-Around dozed off.

Baby hummed a little bedtime tune,
and Bubbles and Wag-Around
fell asleep.

Baby looked around.
The whole family
was fast asleep!

She covered them up.
Then Baby went to sleep too.

The Clown-Arounds think that
the best ending to a happy day
is a good night's sleep.
Don't you?

Notes to Grown-ups

Major Themes

Here is a quick guide to the significant themes and concepts at work in *Sweet Dreams, Clown-Arounds!*

- Getting to sleep can sometimes be difficult, as Baby and the rest of the Clown-Arounds found out.
- Loving care: as shown by all the family to Baby, and by Baby to them.
- Acting on impulse: acting quickly without thinking can have surprising results.

Step-by-step Ideas for Reading and Talking

Here are some ideas for further give-and-take between grown-ups and children. The following topics encourage creative discussion of *Sweet Dreams, Clown-Arounds!* and invite the kind of open-ended response that is consistent with many contemporary approaches to reading, including Whole Language:

- Look at the pictures on each page. Some simply

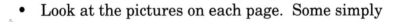

illustrate the words of the text, but some add to it. In particular, what was the trick that Baby played on her parents? Only by looking at the picture can your child understand what the trick was. Ask her or him to say a sentence that tells what Baby did. Write it down. You might even incorporate it into a later telling of the story.

- The Clown-Arounds seem to lead a topsy-turvy life. Look for examples: hanging upside-down, keeping a cake in the closet, making noise to put Baby to sleep, fetching a real animal when Baby was looking at a toy. Examining nonsense can help your child see the importance of using common sense.

Games for Learning

Games and activities can stimulate young readers and listeners alike to find out more about words, numbers, and ideas. Here are more ideas for turning learning into fun:

Slumber Stories

Reading bedtime stories is a classic way to help a child relax and get ready for sweet dreams. But for the child who always seems to want "one more story," parents can successfully use guided meditations to help their child fall asleep. For example,

you can start by telling your child that you will give her or him a pretend story in which he or she is the main character. Dim the lights, play soft, quiet music if you like, and tell your child to close his or her eyes and imagine the following scenario:

- You are in a beautiful, grassy meadow. Look around at the flowers and feel the gentle breeze and the soft sand beneath your feet. Follow the little path to a small, shallow lake. Notice the ripples and the clear color of the water. Lying on smooth stones beneath the water is a small golden box with your name on it. It is small and easy to pick up. Inside is a treasure that is just for you, a treasure that will make you relaxed, safe, and happy. Sit down and open it. Whatever you imagine is inside the box. You can keep the secret treasure in the box or put it in your heart to keep yourself happy and safe.

Then kiss your child good-night.

About the Author
JOANNA COLE, author of the Clown-Around stories, finds herself thinking about these characters often. Ms. Cole was an elementary schoolteacher and a children's book editor before turning to writing full-time. She now writes books for and about children and lives with her family in New York City.

About the Artist
After working in films for many years, JERRY SMATH turned to freelance illustration of children's magazines and textbooks. His work as an illustrator includes such titles as *Get Well, Clown-Arounds!* and *The Clown-Arounds Go On Vacation.* He is also the author/illustrator of *Up Goes Mr. Downs, But No Elephants,* and *Elephant Goes to School.* Mr. Smath lives in Westchester County, New York.